Of Devotion, Heartbreak, and Partings

Cristian Vargas

First Edition — 2025
© 2025 Cristian Camilo Vargas
Mosquera

Writing, editing, and formatting: Cristian
Camilo Vargas Mosquera
Cover design and illustrations: Cristian
Camilo Vargas Mosquera
Proofreading and revision: Cristian
Camilo Vargas Mosquera

Independently published
Printed in the United States of America

ISBN: 979-8-218-83763-1

For the only voice that always said to me,
"Cris, you are capable."
And for those who joined along the way.

Preface

One day I understood that I didn't need to know the exact words for what I felt—that it wasn't necessary to name an emotion or a feeling, because I had other ways to express myself. I could describe what I felt, I could draw with words what my mind lived and what my body experienced. One day I realized that I could translate with words what I sensed, and that could be more precise than any definition or concept.

For a long time, I allowed hundreds of voices that weren't mine to live in my head, whispering every day that I wasn't capable of anything— that I had no talent, that I would never achieve anything. For many years, those voices became my conscience, my constant company: the ones that made me fall, the ones that led me into danger. Voices of people who once hurt me and decided to stay, reminding me to remain silent and submissive, that I couldn't shine, decide, live a life of my own, or even be happy.

I lived in fear, in loneliness, and without the ability to love myself—always pretending to be fine, giving my smile and kindness to everyone, even when they used me, lied to me, or humiliated me. For so long I gave my love only for it to be used, mistreated, and discarded. And through all those years, I wrote what I felt— trying to make poetry, but believing I had no talent at all; believing there was no space in this world, nor in anyone's mind, for someone to want to read what to me were pieces of my soul—the fragments that broke and fell to the ground. I gathered them and joined them again with verses. These poems are not a display of technique or literary skill; they are parts of my story—my pain, my longings, my mistakes, my failures; my doubts and my desire to be loved.

When you read these verses, think of my tears, my sighs; think of the disappointment and confusion of not understanding why love often leaves only wounds behind. Perhaps you'll hear my heartbeat—or smile, imagining how naïve I am.

If you find yourself in any of these words, I hope you know you are not alone—that your will is greater and stronger than they ever made you believe.

With love,
Cristian Vargas

Poems

Devotion

Devotion

I'm a dream caught in your pupils,

and you still don't know

whether to love me now

or miss me later.

I've thought about it—

nine hundred and eleven times.

That I want to love you too,

but I'm all tangled up.

I don't know how to reach you,

how to hold you close—

closer, still closer—

until your air becomes my air,

until your eyelids brush against my skin,

and my sighs escape from your soul

until there's no room left for fear.

I want our minds so near

that words become useless,

too small for something

as simple as "good morning."

I want you near.

I don't want you to leave.

I don't want to turn my back and say goodbye.

Goodbyes are desperate,

waiting is endless,

and thinking of you

never brings you back.

I want to ask

if you'd stay with me for a second—

this close,

this together,

this present.

Maybe the thought makes you smile,

or frown,

or maybe you'll leave in silence—

in a hurry,

or in doubt.

Tell me you want me.

And when our eyes meet,

let the drums roll—

deep, resounding—

in my throat,

and in your hips.

Time burns through me,

seconds slip from my hands.

Don't look at me like that—

I stumble.

When your eyes pierce into mine,

I only want to invent more hours.

Don't turn away.

Look at me.

I can see in your eyes

everything you dreamed last night.

Speak to me.

When you do,

I can taste your words on my tongue.

My pores open to take you in.

Don't laugh like that.

Don't clench your fists.

You take my breath away.

If I sigh, it's from imagining

your time as mine—

that in your mind,

you undress me.

Don't ask.

I want everything you want.

Come closer.

Stay in the sweat you've left on my skin.

And don't ever leave again.

Another First Love

You left me defenseless—

raised your flag,

drove it through my hand,

made me yours by making yourself mine.

Stop chasing ghosts.

Look at me.

Feel me.

Me. Only me.

My castle is made of glass.

Look through it—

through my doors,

my windows.

You can see me. I'm not hiding.

You've crossed my halls,

my bedrooms, my stairs.

You've turned every piece of furniture upside

down

until you found me,

until you had me—

and now you can't let go.

You've already won the battle.

Stop fighting.

Stop searching for more blood,

more pain.

Let me in.

Let me find you.

Let me drown in your scent.

Hold on to me.

The war is over.

Let me in.

Your scent still lives on my skin,

your taste won't leave my lips.

Your name—

your name—

my body calls for it,

my breath whispers it.

My eyes keep following you—

when you walk,

when you hide,

when you're gone.

Even in the shadows I search for you,

among sparks, among whispers.

I search for you.

I call you.

I miss you.

You dor —

my hand isn't my han

I search for you in my words.

Collapse

You can't see everything I feel,

though I burn with the fever of thinking of you,

and can't find warmth anywhere

but in your arms.

My eyes can't stop seeing you,

my lips whisper your name all day.

You don't feel my hands

reaching for you,

though you're not here.

The ground still remembers your steps.

I want to see you walk in.

I want you near.

I want you to be mine.

Because I'm used to hiding.

Because I've only ever known goodbye.

Because I've never been enough.

Because there's always been someone else.

I want you to see what I feel,

but I hide.

I want you to see that I care,

but I cover it with laughter.

I want you to feel my affection,

my desire,

my need.

I want to cover you,

surround you,

fill you,

so that you'll never lack anything,

so that you'll always find me,

so you'll have no reason

not to choose

me.

Lovers Without Breath

You feel it:

pure, near, pulsing —

the breath of a man already condemned,

a love-lost wanderer exhaling;

the sigh of death,

the decay of bodies,

my soul burning in life's own hell,

existing without seeing

the hunger in your clouded eyes.

You exhale.

Slowly, while staying tense,

you pull in distant longings,

your mind filled

with the scent of wet sex,

with the fear

of not being eternal.

You exhale harder.

You feel life

and slip away,

hide in the wind,

cling to the light.

Streetlamps reflect in your pupils.

You know you'll turn to dry branches,

to a stone that doesn't move —

yet you can still hear it:

how it rises from the pit of your stomach,

how you haven't forgotten

the tremor of my flesh,

weak and reckless before you.

You're running out of air.

You know the axe

never waits for three.

Hallelujah

I know you don't believe

in gods or saints.

You aren't blinded by virgins

of pure desire

or burning prayers.

The flesh is your heaven;

in the heat of your victim

you raise your praise.

You mock life

with every suicidal attempt,

you laugh

at those who fall in love.

I know you don't love —

pleasure is your sacrament,

everything is passion and hunger.

And yet...

I crave your arms and your chest,

to die by your hands,

to die with my throat open.

I plunged into Acheron,

searching for your indifference,

thirsting for the salt of your body.

I drank your death,

I tasted your blood.

Now you see your own creation.

Now I see your heaven.

My eyes are open

to your resurrection

in my pupils.

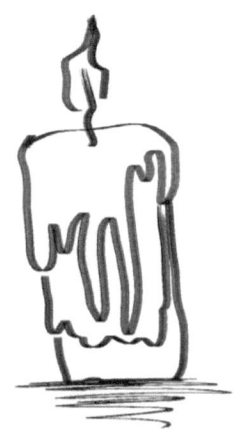

Prayer

Submissive, bowed, contrite,
I come to you in awe,
trembling before your greatness.
I understand your silence,
the pain I've endured
for daring to live free.
I prepare for the wake —
all will dress in mourning,
resigned to grief;
but in the midst of sobs
the lovers will tumble,
the only flowers blooming
from their hunger.
No hymn or prayer can silence
the sublime song
of lust.
Drunk with pleasure, my lord,
I'll lean against the gravestone,
tear my clothes,
and with every thrust
cry out your epitaph.

Look at Me Again

I will follow the eternal soul,

the god of my madness.

I will love your body —

that immortal victim —

and cry drops of its perfume.

Then I'll avenge the fallen:

his loneliness,

his innocence,

his rage.

Now dry leaves fall,

the ones from your spring.

The wind scattered your ashes,

and turned to storm.

Confusion caught me.

The air stumbles in and out.

How long have I been laughing?

It was all a bad joke.

They look at me with pity —

like a starving, filthy cat.

They don't know I'm dying,

drying out,

the pain crawling up my throat.

Look at me once more.

Ignore me once more.

Let me lose myself in the dense forests,

without path or end,

that opened before me,

that closed behind me.

I want to drown in that blind lake

bathed in tears —

where a sadder, but truer world

reflected itself.

Look at me again.

I haven't finished loving you.

Tell me the reflection hasn't faded —

the image of my naked body

in the perfect glass of your eyes.

Let my throat bathe once more.

Give me to drink your essence, your scent.

Feed me once more.

Love me once more.

There will be time to die later.

Heartbreak

A Casual Visit

I trace the shape of your darkness,

cling to your silence,

touch softly the outline of you…

Absence.

In the void of your love

I search in vain for the pulse of our time —

but nothing sounds.

Silence.

Still, I hold on, I don't let go —

then I fall.

Have you gone?

Sadness wears my skin;

I've become a meow in the night.

I remember your warmth —

that gentle, secret pink.

You find me.

My lips open,

and you fill me with your universe.

You breathe fast; you don't look at me.

These few minutes

are all the life I'll ever have.

You tremble in silence.
You seem satisfied, but
I never heard it —
the beating in your chest.
Are you still there?
I turn to kiss you—
but only your scent lingers,
your trace still damps upon my skin.

Seduction

The sky slips down,

I breathe the agony of the clouds —

red, clinging to life.

His gaze is lost, my reason gone.

I can hear his heartbeat

from the other side of the bed.

I love him.

His hand stretches out,

almost brushing me.

I caress his jaw —

my fingers touch the world:

one with more blood, more heat.

I feel his face, I move toward his hips.

He shudders, looks at me, and I burn.

He comes closer — I don't flee, I tremble.

He pours fire over my barren valleys.

My mind dies,

while life sings,

while our bodies sing.

Never was I so close to the infinite —

the eternity of the universe

in his lips.

His body, his thirst, his hunger.

Never had I drunk the spirit of the universe.

Never had I felt life so near my skin —

except in that afternoon

when we abandoned the cosmos.

He filled my shameful emptiness

with his rivers,

and showed me a sea

without bottom,

without shores —

so alive, so violent

it claimed my body until nightfall.

I begged to drown in that sea,

for after him,

who else could inhabit my oceans?

Hunter

You carry a gaze of threat.

Each step you take

echoes the steps of my death.

I see you —

my blood rushes into boiling,

heat rising to the idea of your desire.

You hear the ants stir,

you sense the wind's desire.

And before you:

my hollow body,

waiting.

Your eyes fix on me.

You watch illusions bloom,

mushrooms in the forest,

branches sprouting from a dead trunk —

dreams that you might be mine.

They rise, dark and naïve,

roses opening in the depths of your stare,

silent and intoxicating.

Do you see me?

Are you speaking to me?

The question trembles out,

like a whisper

from your willing prey.

Song

A sad melody,

remains of two lovers.

They move in sorrow,

from key to key.

Each line betrays.

Where silence waits.

No one bends,

no intent to forgive.

The lover ascends.

She watches —

sound pressed

to her lips.

Time holds its breath.

The notes collapse.

He steps.

He falls.

A sigh.

A kiss.

The violin shatters.

Applause.

No beginning matters.

They performed for the plot.

The curtain drops.

Only silence remains.

Falsehood

In absolute emptiness,

inside this world of two,

I feel alone,

and I am alone —

a fragile ghost.

We dance to the rhythm of madness.

We dressed the darkness.

There's no beauty to the touch —

we, impostors, chasing love.

He doesn't know who I am,

yet he kissed me.

He told me shiny lies.

I can hide my fears, my vanity,

my hope, my faith,

until he got me laid.

All is dance.

Time fades to nothingness.

No more above,

there's no ground.

We move between mirrors.

Neither of us knows

which side we dance on.

Sheets of Color

I dreamed

a blue butterfly,

the whiskers of a kitten,

and a drop of blood.

I cry, tearing at silence.

I've torn this infamous skin,

sown a field

of red tulips.

Everything is so beautiful.

The room begins to dance,

colors begin to fade.

A frost burned the flowers.

My body turns to sand.

I vanish.

I can't find my voice.

My feet no longer dance.

Forget Again

I walked in the shadow

of a blinding light,

and there you were —

a ghost out of prayer,

a ghost stitched to my memory.

Your jade eyes,

your lips belonging to no one.

The blue sound of your words.

With every step you grew brighter.

I no longer saw your face,

I no longer felt your hands.

I forgot that I loved you,

or perhaps that I hated you.

I no longer knew your name.

I didn't know

what was vanishing before me.

I stepped forward —

like you never did.

One Word

I saw your eyes behind the clouds.

Now I look down to the ground.

I catch your glimpse,

my mind's unhinged.

All words collapse into one,

divine and yet profound:

your name,

your name,

your name.

I raised my glass, for you were gone.

I gulped my tears, I tore no more

my sacred feelings,

your absence-love.

Denial

I notice the single tear,

dripping down to damp

the wounds of despair.

I hear the faint weep,

as soft as the crash

of an eyelash falling.

I see your life,

missing all its colors —

stars without light

on your tired skin.

I see the foam,

white and floating

upon the waves.

They sway and fade

like your mind.

I watch you wander lost,

churning the barren ground,

digging deep

into lapsed memory.

My silence breaks.

You scream your nonsense,

forgetting that I watch you

from the other side
of your madness.

By Your Side

I found our dreams —

our dying dreams —

upon your pillow.

My soul clings to your tomorrows,

to every tomorrow —

always passing, never coming —

that we never lived.

I live my autumn,

breathing the colors I imagined.

I dream my life — and yours,

my hollow lover.

I have no words.

I have no prayers.

I contemplate the world,

all that is beautiful and pure.

I exhale —

while you

rise

and close the door.

Pretend You Care

Stay silent —

I'm feeling the pain your words left.

Stay silent —

I'm carrying our past on my back.

Wait until I'm gone.

Fake your affliction.

Act like it hurts.

Think of my smile.

Then return

to your freedom.

Reminiscences After the Fall

Love me!

See me — I'm real,

I don't lie.

This is who I am,

here I am,

transparent,

entirely yours.

So transparent you stopped seeing me,

so real you struggled to believe it,

so sincere I was never enough.

But this is me:

the fruit that bled in your mouth,

the garden that bloomed at your whim.

It's me,

the one who slept in your clouds,

who believed in every future —

uncertain, magical,

a thousand lives together.

I'm the one who stayed,

so you could break my spirit.

That was me, the one you smiled at,

the one you kissed,

the one you made feel special.
I'm the one you shattered,
the one you wounded with ease,
the one who was never enough.
I am the pieces left behind,
after you.

Expectations

Through the window I watch you,

the glass of your doubts between us,

wrapped in noise,

my blood leaps and pleads.

I observe you,

my eyes know you in detail.

Everything in you is perfect.

The light reflects on your mouth,

your lips open.

You give me life.

I blush,

you laugh and step away.

In silence I call you,

I beg you to be mine.

You don't turn around.

I will wait for you to return,

to water again the gardens

of my barren pelvis.

I Write to You

It is law, my love,

to love you.

My hands have learned

to seek your body,

and my eyes to seek your eyes.

My moments of pleasure

live in the secrecy of your lips,

and in your cruel caresses.

You are not breeze, nor ice,

not rock, nor fire, nor sea.

You are a note —

a verse in the void.

I wander

the odyssey of your absence,

longing that you might love me,

even though

my letters always go without a name.

Partings

Transmutation

You chose to die,

you grew tired of life,

of music and lies.

Therefore, I'm sadness.

I miss your absence, your silence.

Everything is so white, and so black.

I remember you —

sailing a sky of anguish, loneliness,

and despair.

I sigh and I weep — you were a strand of God.

I remember and I weep — the veil of a virgin.

I hate and I weep — the perfume of a whore.

I still wait for you to rise again.

I sang in silence

beside your withered body. I did not leave the

coffin.

And you do not return.

The glass keeps me from your lips

that still seem drenched with the blood of a

betrayed Christ,

from your eyes as closed as God's ears,

from your being, as absent as always.

There you are, inert,
surrounded by the repentant, the ashamed,
and by a cursed one —
one who still lives in your memory,
one who will live to love you in hell.

Waiting at the Same Hour

I wish I had never seen your eyes:

green, alive, invincible —

so I wouldn't have to see them now, closed,

lifeless.

I wish I had never noticed your lips,

those fields soaked in war —

so I wouldn't have to see them now, pale with

death.

I wish I had never heard your voice,

so I wouldn't be missing it,

searching for it in the music you once loved.

I wish away the paths we walked together,

but now my tears harden on the pavement.

I long to be strong, not to cry,

but my breath died on your lips.

I want to stop dreaming.

I want to wake up.

I still write to you.

I am still poisoned by your memory.

I am sadness — and sadness reminds me of you.

I still wait for you to walk beside me,

plucking petals from a flower I wait for you,

but...

you no longer arrive.

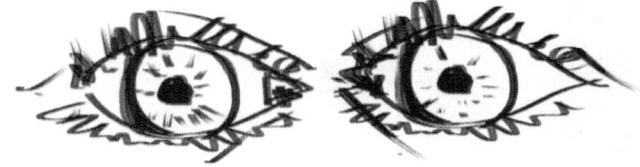

Italics

The saddest sound
is none other than
the last breath of silence.
The surrender of lips
after an unrestrained kiss.
The brush of skin
after the soft touch
of goodbye.

Broken Threads

I escape from life,

it chases me, and I run.

All taken from me,

I am lighter than life itself.

I will no longer be who I was,

nor who I never was.

I run from myself, I run from the world,

forget rage,

forget love and fear.

I will no longer be a shadow

moved by threads in the dark.

I am the memory of my own forgetting,

a leaf sliding in the wind.

They see me fall and scream,

yet I feel one with the air.

At the sound of my goodbye, they cried —

those who never heard my silences.

No one understands, however,

the endless fall of the one who jumps,

and how the one who leaps into the void

never lands.

And what are seconds,

but nothing at all?

My Temple

I rise,

cross myself for the last time,

walk through porcelain saints,

their laments, their pleas —

behind me I leave the masks of regret.

I hear the trumpets,

chalices spilling over.

No lash will strike me again,

no wood will hold me.

I drink the blood,

not as salvation

but as intoxication —

the blood that stains the saints' robes,

that fills the coffers

of heaven's heirs.

From the pulpit they condemn me —

eternal fire.

And I answer with my devotion:

not to their God,

but to your lips,

your body,

the scent between your thighs.

Time is reborn.

The doors open.

And at the end of the nave,

desire rises —

and I see God.

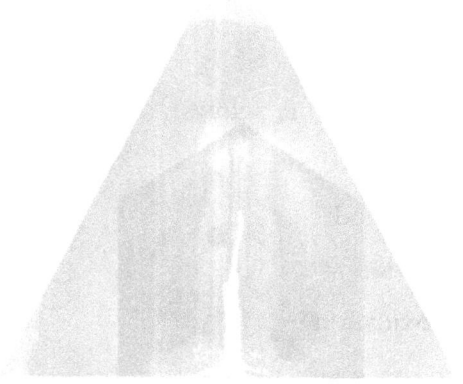

Meditation

I search for you in silence,

looking in the waters

of dying wishing fountains.

I lose your trace,

trying to find you

in the garden

of my madness.

There, between the flowers,

I found you,

and I praised your beauty —

my idea of you.

Existences

I walk.

My eyes taste the leaves,

stroke the tree —

it's being simple,

perfect.

I search for myself in the breeze,

I am only a body,

dust unmoored, falling.

Lost in the wings of a bee,

dreaming inside the dream of a flower,

surrounded by white, quiet stones.

Today I walk, tomorrow I die.

I die in the blast of a star —

light, dust, silence.

In the void: solitude.

A blink, and I exist.

A blink, and I die.

I was the All.

I was the Nothing.

To Live?

It wasn't me —

I don't hold the dagger of irony.

—The heart trembles—

This life is not worth living.

—The thread pulls tight—

My only faith is death:

ridiculous, radiant, precious.

—The scissors close—

Life converges

in its ascension to death.

Prophecy

I went to bed early…

when I woke, my world was at war.

Chaos everywhere.

The news ran red with blood.

The streets had turned into killing fields.

Bullets silenced the people.

Bullets cut down those who fought:

those who fought just to stand,

those who fought to live one day more,

those who fought not to die of hunger,

or of cold,

those who had nothing and still fought,

those who fought because everything

was taken from them.

I woke to the cries of mothers,

the cries of children weeping in panic,

the cries of the dying.

The world around me went dark,

the sky itself drenched in blood.

Mourning voices rose for justice.

Voices begged for help.

But they would not be heard.

Those who should have been heroes

pointed their guns,

fired without mercy.

There were no heroes left.

The flag burned —

in flames, in tears, in blood.

And no one

was willing to forget.

Short Steps, Shorter Paths

You — my companion,

of brief distances and small journeys.

Leaping like a cricket,

from one branch

to another.

Our words walk beside us,

weaving worlds

inside each other's minds.

Inexorable.

We Walk.

I feel complete.

I hear your laughter,

the ringing of your lashes.

I see your face in the sun's rays,

sadness hidden

in rosebuds.

We tread on anecdotes,

steps, laughter,

and silences.

Your mind always adrift,

shipwrecked in doubt,

le, made of pa

ad, the bodies

Insomnia

Like a stolen bird,

not knowing your name,

the night is foreign to me.

Stretched on a mattress of desire,

I sink into the scent of memory,

the memory of your body.

Darkness reveals your eyes.

I count your lashes, one by one.

I trace the map of your iris,

and each night I lose myself

in the lie of your allure.

Gloom

I wrestle with a soul

full of silence,

entirely made of agony.

I wipe my sadness,

raise my arms,

and allow myself to flight.

I am feather,

I am wind —

rising higher,

away from the fear,

from the torment

within me.

My feathers are made of glass,

colored by the shades

of endless regret.

I fly higher,

I can almost reach you,

so elevated,

farther than ever.

There's a blue space

between us —

dividing

I try to move closer.

And you

Mourning

You leave my side,

migrating to another sky,

forgetting that I love you.

But it doesn't matter.

You no longer exist.

You no longer live.

I no longer hear your voice.

I don't find you in the silence.

Your absence does not wound me,

because you were never nearby.

Fading

You left my side,

migrating to another sky,

you left my love behind.

But does it matter?

You have faded,

you have vanished.

I scream your name,

and the silence screams back.

This wound still remembers —

you were never here.

Ascension

I hear a sonata —

I'm ascending to death.

Everything shines brighter,

everything feels lighter.

A scent fills my chest,

memories wet my eyes.

Life burns higher,

and higher as I die.

I have met death in this encounter,

I clung to its warmth.

I feel its blood in my body,

and my body feels its grip.

I feel closer, I feel nearer —

to heaven, to abyss,

to eternity.

And time persists,

lasting longer

than the longest kiss.

Death withdraws.

You take the blade

and step away.

cold,

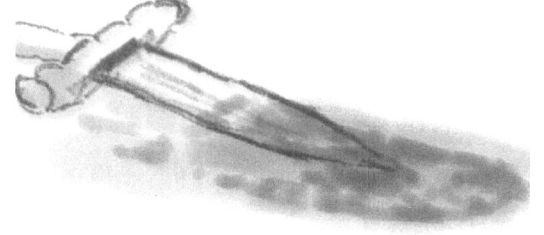

Eternal

I die —

of loneliness, of anguish.

I die —

on the eyelids of the night,

in the secrets kept

by benches in the park.

I die —

for I have dressed the day

and worn the night.

I die —

in the infinity you spilled

over my body:

the heat, the scent, the damp.

I die —

in the mountains, the valleys, the pines,

on the back of a beast.

I die forever, I die.

And it feels like exploding,

like creating a new universe.

Invariable

I am an entity,

motionless, parallel to the world.

Life moves, and leaves me—

I remain trapped

in time and space.

My mind drifts,

my spirit soars,

but this body anchors me,

it lingers, it stalls.

I sink into life,

yet never feel alive.

I will think of a proper end.

Until then,

I'll keep the final point

in my pocket.

Identity

I walk deserted streets,

between shoes scattered on the pavement,

and tires abandoned on the road.

I walk among savage noises,

and scents in black and white.

And I sit to observe:

lips kissing in the air,

anonymous smiles,

winks that drift.

Cigarettes pass smoke

from mouth to mouth,

tears of sorrows not my own.

I search for myself in what's outside me.

Something known.

Something familiar.

I search for my reflection.

I search for nostalgia.

I search for your disdain.

Work of Your Hands

I dream of your hands,

I dream you make me,

that you shape me.

You mold me as time molds life.

I exist between your fingers,

like fruit hidden among leaves.

In my dreams you are the world —

the fleeting,

the eternal.

In my world you are my dreams —

illogical,

perfect.

I wake, floating in the void,

asking what I am,

if I still exist.

I search for eyes

to see me,

to speak to me.

And I think of yours —

watching me in desperation,

desiring me

when desire shakes you.

ting me,

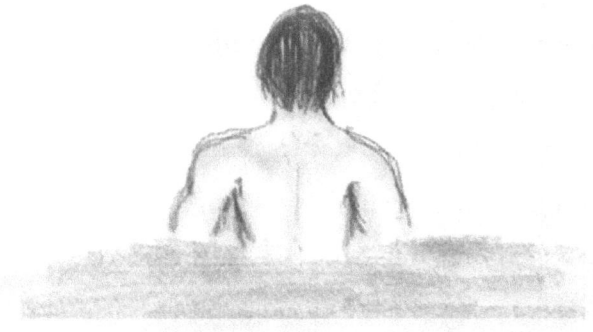

Oblique and Parallel

I should have understood you were gone.

But I kept waiting for your message.

You were gone. Your goodnight message.

You were gone. Telling me to dream sweetly.

You were gone. And no message arrived.

You were gone. And I never wrote you.

You were gone. You wouldn't read that I liked
seeing you.

You were gone. That I would miss you.

You were gone. Because I loved the time.

You were gone. Even if it was short.

You were gone. Even if it was long.

You were gone. That I needed more kisses.

You were gone. That I didn't want to let go of
your arms.

You were gone. Nor forget your scent.

You were gone. And that my leg loved the
weight of your hand.

You were gone.

You are gone.

Final

My tears succumb,

they die on my cheeks,

they will no longer die on your lips.

I will be cradled by misfortune,

by this cursed generation,

by coals burning

in cauldrons

hungry for life.

And I will sing, like a whisper,

like the flutter of a moth.

I will be roses on a pagan altar:

dry petals, dry tears,

ancient blood,

of some brothel messiah.

Now I breathe only the smoke

of my soul in flames,

of my life in flight.

Now I am incense,

I am libation,

wine poured to the setting sun.

I curl into silence,

to speak your name.

About the Author

When my therapist asked me about my dreams, I hesitated for a moment before remembering that, since childhood, my greatest love had always been books. The fascination I have felt for stories, fiction, and novels has always been my safe place. I believe that if I think of a genuinely peaceful and happy episode in my life, it always takes me back to a moment of reading. Whether driven by curiosity, the desire to learn something new, or simple distraction, literature has most often been the force that awakened and stirred that flame in the center of the chest we call spirit.

So, my answer was: my dream is to be a writer.

I was born in Colombia, in a city nestled in the heart of the Andes Mountain range. Fortunately, I never lost the wonder and admiration for the majestic mountains that embrace Ibagué, in the Department of Tolima. Although as a child I lived for a time in different regions of the country, most of my childhood—and everything that comes when people stop calling you a child— took place in Ibagué. I was raised within a somewhat narrow, Christian worldview, but it never quenched my enthusiasm for learning anything that might spark my curiosity.

One of the things I hold dearest in my heart is that I always had books available and within reach. I was that child who, during free periods at school, would go straight to the library, to the point where the librarian remembered your name and recognized you among so many others. That child grew up, was filled with doubts, and had many questions—some of which I am still answering. And, of course, he began to search for himself, to dig out from under countless expectations, ideas, and beliefs, and to understand that you are not what others say you are.

My path led me to study law, and more than a degree in law, I found people who earned my love and loyalty. At the same time, I rediscovered a passion that had become "normal" or routine: I returned to books, fiction, micro fiction, and poetry. I began to read more, attended literary gatherings, and started to write. I have written over and over again erasing, discarding, and starting anew. I have written to heal, to give voice to my essence. Literature, books, and writing have sustained me when I didn't know who I was: through grief and desolation, through changes and new beginnings.

Writing has been one of the most fascinating— and, I must say, dangerous—experiences for anyone afraid of truly knowing themselves. I believe my most honest moments have been these: reading and writing. They allow a level of connection with your inner self that is both deeply complex and profoundly beautiful. So, if something can feel especially difficult, it is recognizing oneself as a writer. Yet it is inevitable: anyone who loves writing eventually comes to accept that the title of writer is not granted by a university or a publisher, but by the natural— almost divine—need to create through words.

Today, the United States is my home. I have begun to choose my own paths, to live according to my own expectations and dreams. I have remembered how to love myself. I have remembered that I can choose happiness, and that I can write the life I want to live.

www.ingramcontent.com/pod-product-compliance
Lightning Source LLC
Chambersburg PA
CBHW050311260626
47156CB00005B/1753